Meghan
e Wedding Sparkle
Fairy

To Irina, who sparkles with magic

Special thanks to
Rachel Elliot

ORCHARD BOOKS

First published in Great Britain in 2018 by The Watts Publishing Group

1 3 5 7 9 10 8 6 4 2

© 2018 Rainbow Magic Limited.
© 2018 HIT Entertainment Limited.
Illustrations © Orchard Books 2018

HiT entertainment

A CIP catalogue record for this book is available from the British Library.

ISBN 978 1 40835 664 7

Printed and bound in Great Britain by CPI Group (UK) Ltd, Croydon, CR0 4YY

MIX
Paper from
responsible sources
FSC® C104740

The paper and board used in this book are made from wood from responsible sources

Orchard Books
An imprint of Hachette Children's Group
Part of The Watts Publishing Group Limited
Carmelite House, 50 Victoria Embankment, London EC4Y 0DZ

An Hachette UK Company
www.hachette.co.uk
www.hachettechildrens.co.uk

Meghan
the Wedding Sparkle Fairy

by Daisy Meadows

ORCHARD

www.rainbowmagic.co.uk

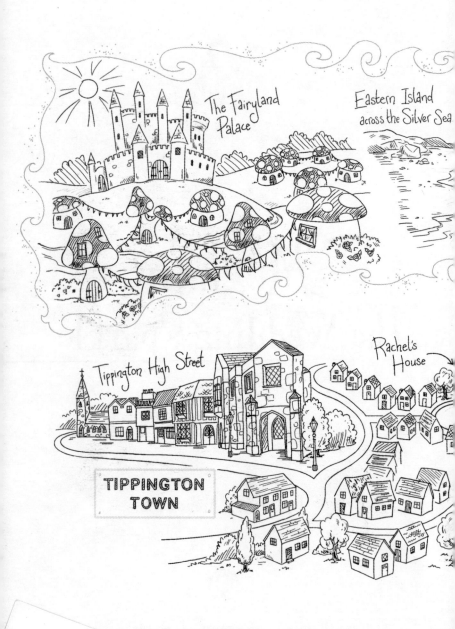

The Fairyland Palace

Eastern Island across the Silver Sea

Tippington High Street

Rachel's House

TIPPINGTON TOWN

Jack Frost's Ice Castle

Tippington Park

Jack Frost's Spell

Meghan's ring makes weddings shine,
So I will make its magic mine!
I'll steal the ring to make quite sure
The spell of love will be no more.

The added bonus, you will see,
Is that the ring will work for me;
Bring luck to all my naughty schemes,
And spoil the fairies' soppy dreams!

Contents

A Surprising Engagement

"My turn," said Rachel Walker.

She threw a shuttlecock up in the air, and then hit it with her racket, sending it flying towards her best friend, Kirsty Tate.

"Good shot!" called Kirsty as she leapt into the air, trying to hit the shuttlecock back with her own racket.

The girls were spending the spring

half-term holiday together at Rachel's
house in Tippington. It was a sunny day
and they had come to the town park for
a game of badminton.

Rachel hit a wild shot and the
shuttlecock disappeared behind a tree.

"Oh!" exclaimed a surprised voice.

Rachel and Kirsty raced around the
tree. On the other side, a young woman
was sitting on a checked picnic blanket.
She was surrounded by screwed-up pieces
of paper, and the shuttlecock was in her
lap. She looked up at the girls, laughing.

"Well, that was unexpected!" she said.

"We're really sorry," said Rachel,
taking the shuttlecock back. "I hit it too
hard."

"That's OK," said the young woman.
"I'm quite glad to have a reason to stop."

"What are you writing?" Kirsty asked.

"I'm trying to write my wedding vows," the young woman said. "But it's not going very well. I'm getting married here in the park and I thought it would be the perfect place to come and write my vows. I had lots of ideas this morning, but now I can't think of a single thing to say."

"Good luck," said Rachel. "I hope you

find the perfect words."

The girls said goodbye and walked away.

"Let's go and get some ice cream," said Kirsty.

They headed across the park towards the café and joined the ice-cream queue. They were behind a young couple who were having a quarrel.

"Our wedding's not going to have any sparkle," the woman was saying. "Just do what I want."

"We're not having purple bows on the chairs," snapped the man. "They have to be orange."

"Orange would look ridiculous," the woman retorted.

"I'm not in the mood for ice cream any more," said the man.

He stomped off, and the woman followed him.

"Goodness," said Kirsty. "It doesn't seem to be a very good day for engaged couples."

She bought a caramel ice cream, and Rachel chose mint chocolate chip. They walked down towards the pond, licking their ice creams. On the way they passed a young couple who were arguing about

the wording of their wedding invitations.

"I wonder why all these people are so cross with each other," said Rachel.

The girls found a grassy spot beside the pond and walked over there to finish their ice creams, watching pond skaters skimming across the water.

"Can you see something sparkling over there?" asked Kirsty suddenly. The sunlight was glittering on something among the reeds opposite. Then a squawking chuckle echoed across the water, and Rachel and Kirsty exchanged a worried look. They would know that sound anywhere.

"That was a goblin," said Rachel.

The girls had shared many magical adventures with their fairy friends, and had often had to defend them from the dastardly deeds of naughty Jack Frost and his goblin servants. The girls both gasped and raced around the pond.

When they pushed the reeds apart, they saw a small huddle of goblins.

"What are you doing here?" Kirsty asked.

The goblins jumped back, and Rachel and Kirsty gasped. Jack Frost was sitting in the middle with a large diamond ring on one of his bony fingers.

Jack Frost glared at the girls, his spiky beard quivering.

"What do you nosy parkers want?" he asked.

Rachel and Kirsty glanced at each other, thinking the same thing. The ring didn't look as if it belonged to him. It contained three beautiful diamonds, the central diamond slightly bigger than the others. The diamonds glittered beautifully in the spring sunshine.

"We'd like to know where you got that ring from,"

said Rachel. "Is it yours?"

Jack Frost went purple with rage.

"Of course it's mine!" he shouted. "It's my engagement ring!"

Jack Frost's Spell

Rachel and Kirsty stared at Jack Frost in amazement.

"Who are you going to marry?" Kirsty asked.

"I'm not marrying anyone," snapped the Ice Lord. "But now I've stolen – er, I mean – got this ring, I'm going to use its magic to make everything go my way."

He stuck out his tongue at the girls,
and then raised his wand. There was a
flash of blue lightning, and then he and
the goblins disappeared. Rachel clutched
her best friend's hand.

"I bet he's stolen that ring from one of
the fairies," she said.

"We have to warn the king and queen,"

said Kirsty.

They crouched down among the reeds and opened the lockets that hung around their necks. Inside each one was a pinch of fairy dust – just enough for one trip to Fairyland.

"On the count of three ..." said Rachel. "One, two, three!"

They sprinkled themselves with sparkling fairy dust. Instantly, they shrank to fairy size and the reeds towered above them. Their filmy wings unfolded and glimmered in the sunlight. At the same time, the reeds curved around them to make a smooth, green cocoon.

"It's like being inside a carriage," said

Rachel in delight.

The reeds shaped themselves into seats, and the girls sat down. Shimmering, sparkly fairy dust surrounded them, and they felt the reed carriage lifting them into the air, bobbing on the wind like a feather. After a few moments, with a gentle bump, the carriage landed. The fairy dust slowly dissipated, and then the reeds unfurled like petals. Rachel and Kirsty peered out and saw that they were in the garden of the Fairyland Palace.

"Rachel and Kirsty, what a wonderful surprise," said a warm

23

voice.

Queen Titania was standing there, smiling at them. The girls curtsied.

"Thank you, Your Majesty,"

said Rachel.

"You've arrived on an exciting day,"
said the queen. "King Oberon's cousin,
Prince Gareth, is getting married in a
few hours. The wedding will be here in
the palace garden, so everyone is very
busy."

"How lovely," said Kirsty, gazing
around at the white-lily arches and
silvery stars that decorated the garden.
"Who is Prince Gareth marrying?"

"Princess Kate of the Eastern Island,"
said the queen. "It's far away on the other
side of the Silver Sea. But what brings
you to Fairyland?"

"I'm afraid we're here because of Jack
Frost," said Rachel.

Quickly, she explained what they had
seen among the reeds. Queen Titania

frowned.

"I think I know who owns that ring," she said.

The queen shook her wand and it tinkled like a bell. Kirsty and Rachel were delighted to see their friends Kate the Royal Wedding Fairy and Mia the Bridesmaid Fairy flying towards them. The fairies smiled at them and curtsied

to the queen.

"You called us, Your Majesty?" Kate asked.

"I'm afraid that Jack Frost is causing trouble for the wedding," said Queen Titania. "Rachel and Kirsty have travelled here to warn us."

"We have been having some problems," Mia admitted.

"What sort of problems?" asked the queen.

Kate took a deep breath. "The order of service cards have all gone blank, the lilies have wilted, the 'something old' is missing, the bridesmaids'

dresses have all changed into fancy-dress
costumes, the prince can't remember
what the wedding dance song is supposed
to be and no one can find the king's
wedding speech."

"Meghan the Wedding Sparkle Fairy
has been working hard to give this
wedding extra-special sparkle," said Mia.
"But it's almost as if her spell of love has
stopped working."

Queen Titania turned to Mia and Kate.

"Will you take our guests to the palace
to find Meghan?" she asked. "I think Jack
Frost may have stolen something from
her."

"We'll help however we can," said
Kirsty.

"Thank you," said the queen.
"Fairyland can always count on you."

The four fairies swooped up to the palace and into the throne room. It was bustling with fairies, frog footmen and decorations.

"Has anyone seen Meghan?" asked Kate.

"She was in the east tower room earlier," called one of the wedding workshop fairies.

The east tower room door was locked.

"Meghan, are you there?" called Mia, knocking.

"Yes!" said a muffled voice. "Please help!"

Kate tapped her wand on the lock, and the door flew open. In the middle of the room, a fairy with wavy, dark hair was sitting on a wooden chair. She was wearing a long white wraparound dress with a delicate lace front. Her wings were fluttering helplessly, and her wand was lying on the floor.

"Jack Frost trapped me here with a sticky spell," she cried. "I can't move!"

The Ice Castle Gardens

With a wave of Mia's wand, the spell was broken. Meghan jumped off the chair and picked up her wand.

"Thank you," she said. "I thought I was going to be stuck there all day."

"Rachel and Kirsty, this is Meghan the Wedding Sparkle Fairy," said Kate. "Meghan, what happened?"

"Jack Frost sneaked in disguised as a wedding cake baker," Meghan said. "When I bent down to look in the cake box, he knocked my wand out of my hand and cast his spell. It was like being frozen to the chair. I couldn't stop him from taking my magical engagement ring from the chain around my neck."

"What does your ring do?" Rachel asked.

"It helps me to look after the magic of matrimony everywhere," Meghan explained. "As long as I wear the ring, my spell of love sprinkles weddings with sparkle."

"It sounds wonderful," said Kirsty.

"It is," said Meghan. "But without my ring, the spell of love is broken and the wedding sparkle has disappeared from the human and fairy worlds. All the little details that make weddings perfect – the first dance, the invitations, the decorations – are going wrong, and love itself will start to fade. Couples everywhere will start falling out and forgetting what they love about each other."

Quickly, Kirsty and Rachel told

Meghan about seeing Jack Frost in the park.

"May we help you get your ring back?" asked Rachel.

"Yes please!" said Meghan, clasping her hands together.

"Mia and I will look after things here," said Kate.

She blew a kiss to Rachel and Kirsty, and then swooped out of the room with Mia behind her.

"I can't understand why Jack Frost would do something so mean," said Meghan.

"We can," said Rachel, remembering their past adventures with Kate and Mia.

"He doesn't like weddings
because he thinks
they're silly and
soppy, so anything
that he can do
to spoil them will
make him happy."

"Yes, and he does
like magic and power,
and the ring is full of
both," added Kirsty.

"My ring will make sure that
everything around him has a little bit of
extra sparkle," said Meghan. "A touch
of luck here, a sprinkle of excitement
there – it will make everything shine a
little brighter and seem a little better.
So as long as the ring is with Jack
Frost, everything will go his way – and

weddings will continue to go badly!"

"Then we have to get your ring back before the start of the royal wedding," said Rachel. "First stop, the Ice Castle."

Flying high above the green hills, Rachel and Kirsty could see how much the whole of Fairyland had been looking forward to the royal wedding. Banners

and bunting were draped between the
toadstool houses, and every hilltop had
a party table piled high with cupcakes,
sandwiches, fruit and sweets.

"We can't let the fairies down," said
Rachel, squeezing her best friend's hand.
"This wedding deserves all the sparkle a
royal wedding can have."

Kirsty nodded, and pointed ahead
to where the Ice Castle stood. The air
was suddenly chilly, and the clouds had
grown thick overhead.

"There are no guards on the
battlements," said Kirsty. "Let's fly straight
up there."

"It could be dangerous if we get caught," said Meghan. "I should go by myself."

"No way," said Rachel in a firm voice. "We're staying by your side no matter what."

Meghan flashed her a grateful smile, and a few seconds later they landed on the castle battlements.

"I can't see a single goblin," said Kirsty, peering down into the courtyard below.

"Listen," said Rachel.

They stood very still and listened.
Faintly, they could hear far-off squawks
and squeals.

"The sound is coming from the other
side of the castle," said Meghan.

Together, the three fairies fluttered
towards the noise. Then they stared in
astonishment.

Usually, Jack Frost's garden was empty
and bare, with ice-hard flowerbeds and
leafless branches. But today, it looked
like a winter wonderland. There were
ice slides, sparkling arches made of firs
and snowdrops, fountains of ice-cold
lemonade and crystals dangling from
snowy tree branches, sending rainbow
colours dancing around the garden.

"I never would have imagined that
this gloomy place could look so

beautiful," said Rachel.

"It's the power of the ring's wedding sparkle," said Meghan. "It touches everything with its special magic. The good news is that it means my ring is somewhere nearby."

"And what is the bad news?" asked Kirsty, noticing the worried look in Meghan's eyes.

"It will make things go sparklingly well for whoever is wearing it," said Meghan. "It means that as long as Jack Frost wants to keep the ring, it's going to be very hard to take it from him. All the luck will be on his side."

Kirsty in Disguise

Meghan waved her wand, and a clock face appeared in the air beside them, its golden hands gleaming.

"Princess Kate will be arriving for her wedding in half an hour," she said. "We have to get the ring back in time or her wedding just won't sparkle."

"Don't worry," said Rachel, slipping her

arm around Meghan's waist. "We'll make sure that this is a day to remember for all the right reasons."

The fairies fluttered down and landed on the main path through the gardens.

"Watch out for goblins," said Kirsty.

A crowd of goblins was clambering around each of the lemonade fountains, climbing over

each other to reach the delicious fizzy
drink. Others, full up with lemonade,
were staggering around and hiccupping.

"They're too interested in the lemonade
to notice us," said Rachel.

The girls scrunched over the icy grass,
peering left and right to try to see Jack
Frost. But there was no flash of blue
among the white ice and the green
goblins. They reached the end of the
main path and saw several smaller paths
snaking off from it. Meghan turned to
look at them all.

"Which way?" she asked.

"Look at those trees over there," said
Rachel, pointing. "Do they look extra icy
and sparkly to you?"

"Yes," said Kirsty in an excited voice.
"And the snow underneath them looks

45

extra bright. Could your ring be making
that happen, Meghan?"

"Yes, definitely," Meghan exclaimed.
"Let's go faster!"

They sped along the little path that
led under the dazzling trees. On the way,
they spotted icicles shaped like goblins,

snowdrifts carved into foamy waves and snowflakes frozen against tree trunks like tiny decorations. Then Rachel stopped so suddenly that Meghan and Kirsty bumped into the back of her.

"Look up ahead," she whispered.

They were on the edge of an icy glade, and Jack Frost was stomping around in the centre. Delicate webs of frost had made intricate patterns among the branches. The fairies slipped behind a tree and peered at the Ice Lord.

"Look at his hand," Kirsty said softly.

A large diamond ring was glittering on
his finger.

Jack Frost was scowling and muttering
to himself. Rachel, Kirsty and Meghan
leaned forward to hear what he was
saying.

"It's not fair," they heard him grumble.
"Just because I don't like soppy weddings,
I have to miss out on being the centre
of attention and getting piles of presents.
I want a day like that without all the
disgusting lovey-dovey stuff!"

"He wants a wedding without having
to actually marry someone," said Rachel.

"That gives me an idea," said Kirsty.
"Perhaps there's a way we can trick him
into handing the ring over. Meghan, can
you magic up a mirror in the glade?"

Meghan flicked her wand, and a full-

length mirror appeared in front of Jack
Frost. Instead of glass, it was made of
polished ice, and the frame was frosty
blue.

"Ah, I suppose this is something else my
wonderful new ring can do," said Jack
Frost, smiling at his reflection.

"Now, turn me into Jack Frost," Kirsty
whispered. "I need to make him believe
that I'm his reflection."

Meghan and Rachel looked astonished, but they knew that time was running out. Meghan tapped her wand on Kirsty's head, and her hair turned white and twisted upwards into spikes. A spiky beard sprang from her chin, and her bones became knobbly.

"Good luck," said Rachel.

Jack Frost's True Love

Kirsty tiptoed around the glade and slipped behind the mirror. Then Meghan waved her wand, and the polished ice melted away. Kirsty stepped through the frame and Jack Frost took a step back.

"What's all this?" he demanded.

"I'm your reflection," said Kirsty,

sounding exactly like the grumpy Ice Lord. "The ring wants to make your wishes come true."

"What are you talking about?" Jack Frost snapped.

"You're so clever and handsome," said Kirsty. "No one could ever be incredible enough to deserve to marry you."

Jack Frost gave a pleased smile and ran his hand through his spikes.

"There's only one way that you can marry someone as cunning and gorgeous as you," Kirsty went on. "You'll have to marry yourself."

"That does make sense," said Jack Frost.

"You're marvellous and so am I," said Kirsty. "We were made for each other. We can have a wedding and get masses of presents, just like you want."

"Yes!" Jack Frost exclaimed.

"All you have to do is put the ring on my finger to show that we're engaged," said Kirsty.

She held out her hand, and Jack Frost got down on one knee. Rachel and Meghan peeped out from behind the tree, smiling. But just as he was about to slip the ring on to her finger, he glanced up and saw the fairies.

"No!" he roared.

He shoved Kirsty away from him and

pulled out his wand. With a blue crackle
of icy magic, he broke Meghan's spell.
The mirror disappeared and Kirsty
looked like herself again.

Meghan and Rachel dashed out from
behind the tree and stood bravely either
side of Kirsty.

"You fluttering little fusspots," said Jack Frost with a sneer. "Weedy wimps like you could never trick me into handing over the ring."

"Give it back," said Rachel. "Weddings everywhere will be spoiled without it."

"Good," said Jack Frost. "Why would I give up something that makes everything a little bit better?"

Rachel felt a sudden rush of hope.

"That's it," she said in a whisper. "Maybe we don't need to trick Jack Frost at all. Maybe the ring's magic can make him a little bit better too!"

Rachel stepped forward to stand in

front of Jack Frost. She felt a bit scared,
but she kept thinking about the royal
wedding and all the fairies who were
looking forward to it.

"Today is a really important day," she
said. "Prince Gareth and Princess Kate
are getting married. A wedding should be
perfect and sparkly, and a royal wedding
needs to be even more special."

The magical diamond ring seemed to twinkle.

"Without the ring, it won't be a special day," Rachel went on. "All the little touches that make a wedding like a dream will fail. Meghan needs her ring so she can do her best."

The ring was glimmering now, but Rachel couldn't drag her eyes away from Jack Frost's face. Something amazing was happening to his expression. All the hard spikiness seemed to soften, and the soft shine

57

of the ring was reflected in his eyes.

"The wedding sparkle magic is working," whispered Meghan. "It's working on Jack Frost!"

The Royal Wedding

"Hold out your hand," said Jack Frost to Meghan.

His voice was kind, and Meghan didn't feel afraid. She held out her hand, and he dropped the ring into her palm with a sound like a chiming bell.

Smiling, Meghan waved her wand.

A silver chain appeared, looping itself through the ring and then around her neck. At once, a feeling of love and excitement swept over the girls. Looking at Jack Frost, they could see that he felt it too.

Just then, there was a whooshing sound overhead. They all looked up and saw something white streaking across the sky.

"It's Princess Kate's carriage," said
Meghan. "We don't have much time."

She waved her wand, and the white,
frosty glade disappeared. In the blink of
an eye they were all standing outside the
Fairyland Palace. Jack Frost was wearing
a blue morning suit, and beside him were
four goblins in glittering green pageboy
suits. The king and queen came out of
the palace.

"We are glad to see you, Jack Frost,"
said the queen, taking him by the arm.

Rachel and Kirsty barely had time

to catch their breath before a sparkling white carriage landed in front of them, led by four prancing unicorns.

The door of the carriage opened, and the king stepped forward to help the bride down. She was wearing a gown as white as snow, with a sprinkling of glittering silver stars around the hem.

"Welcome, Princess Kate," said Meghan. "Today is going to be one of the most sparkly, magical days you have ever had."

The princess gave her a happy smile.

"Are you ready?" asked King Oberon.

"I can hardly wait," said Princess Kate.

Meghan took Rachel and Kirsty's hands and led them into the garden, where rows of fairy guests were waiting. They found their seats and watched as Jack Frost led the queen to her throne among the flowers. Then the goblins walked slowly down the aisle, scattering green petals. Behind them, the king and the princess walked towards Prince Gareth, and beautiful music filled the air.

"Look up there," Rachel whispered.

She pointed to a leafy branch where a dove, a bluebird and a lark were singing their hearts out.

"Everything's perfect," said Meghan.

Her diamond ring twinkled on the chain around her neck. Rachel and Kirsty exchanged a happy smile.

"This really is a fairytale wedding," said Kirsty.

After the ceremony, magical confetti swirled around the happy couple and then led the way to a scrumptious picnic in the centre of the garden. When the food was all eaten and the king had made his wonderful speech, the Music Fairies began to play. Prince Gareth and Princess Kate danced around the garden, twirling up into the air

and around the highest branches of the trees, while butterflies swooped around them. Then the king and queen joined the dance, followed by Jack Frost and all four goblins. Soon, the air and the ground were filled with dancers.

"It's been the best wedding ever," said Kirsty, when it was time to go home.

"Thank you for letting us be part of it."

"Thank you for helping me to make it the best wedding ever," said Meghan, hugging them both. "There wouldn't have been any sparkle without you."

She filled their lockets with fairy dust again. Then she waved her wand, and Rachel and Kirsty were

lifted up in a blurry whirl of wedding sparkles. When the glitter faded from their eyes, they were once more standing beside the Tippington Park pond.

The girls picked up their bags and made their way back to the café. Even though no time had passed in the human

world since they had been away, things
were very different. The couples they
had seen quarrelling were walking along
hand in hand, laughing.

"There's the lady who was writing her
vows," said Rachel.

The lady smiled
and waved at the
girls.

"I found the
perfect words,"
she called.

Rachel and
Kirsty waved
back at her.

"It's been
an amazing
adventure," said
Kirsty. "I never

wanted that wedding to end!"

"And it's only day one of half term," said Rachel with a laugh. "I can't wait to find out what the rest of the holiday will bring!"

The End

**Now it's time for Kirsty and
Rachel to help...**

Ellen the
Explorer Fairy

Read on for a sneak peek ...

"I've never had breakfast on a train
before," said Rachel Walker. "It makes
everything taste extra yummy."

She still couldn't believe that they were
halfway around the world. It was only
a day since they had left Wetherbury
and boarded an aeroplane, but it felt like
longer. Now they were sitting on a train,
speeding towards the Congo jungle.

Rachel pressed her nose against the
glass of the dining-car window. The
famous Jungle Express train was speeding

across a vast, flat savannah. She could see mountains in the far distance, and blue-white clouds swirling around their peaks. Rachel turned and smiled at her best friend, Kirsty Tate.

"I still can't believe that we're really here," said Kirsty. "My mum told me that the Jungle Express is one of the most famous trains in the world."

Rachel nodded and picked up a teaspoon to stir her cup of hot chocolate.

"Even the teaspoons are engraved with the Jungle Express emblem," she said.

The girls smiled at each other and sipped their drinks. They were the best hot chocolates either of them had ever tasted.

"Your cousin Margot is so lucky," said Kirsty. "She's only a year older than us, but she has been to some of the most amazing places on the planet."

"That's because Aunt Willow is such a famous explorer," said Rachel. "Every school holiday, she and Margot go adventuring together. We hardly ever see them. Last year they spent the whole summer holiday in the Amazon rainforest. Dad says that the harder a place is to get to, the more Aunt Willow likes it. And this time, we actually get to join them."

"Tell me all about it again," said Kirsty with a wriggle of excitement.

"Aunt Willow has been trying to find the Lost City of the Congo for as long as I can remember," said Rachel. "Now she thinks she has found the map that will lead her there. She said it will be the discovery of a lifetime. We have to take the train to the station on the edge of the Congo jungle and meet an aeroplane that will fly us across to the river. We'll take a boat down the river to a landing place, and then trek to the Lost City."

Kirsty leaned forward over the white tablecloth, her eyes sparkling.

"It's so thrilling," she whispered. "I'm not used to such incredible things happening in the human world."

The girls smiled at each other, thinking about the many magical adventures they had shared with their friends in Fairyland. At that moment, the train started to slow down, and then stopped with a jerk. Teacups rattled in their saucers, and the dining-car waiter lost his balance and wobbled.

"Why are we stopping?" Kirsty asked,

looking out at the empty plain that stretched around them. "This isn't a station."

"The driver seems to be having some trouble with the route this morning," said the waiter. "I expect he's stopping to check that he is on the right track."

Rachel frowned.

"But surely he has done this journey lots of times before?" she asked.

The waiter just shrugged and went to greet some new customers. Seconds later, the train jerked and then set off again. Kirsty took a bite of toast.

Suddenly, the teacup on the saucer next to Kirsty rattled. She looked at it in surprise.

"Are we stopping again?" she asked.

"No," said Rachel in a breathless

whisper. "Look at the cup, Kirsty — it's glowing."

She reached out and turned the teacup the right way up. A tiny fairy was waving up at them from inside.

"Hello," she said in a cheerful voice. "I'm Ellen the Explorer Fairy."

Read Ellen the Explorer Fairy to find out
what adventures are in store for Kirsty and Rachel!

Calling all parents, carers and teachers!
The Rainbow Magic fairies are here to help
your child enter the magical world of reading.
Whatever reading stage they are at, there's
a Rainbow Magic book for everyone!
Here is Lydia the Reading Fairy's guide to
supporting your child's journey at all levels.

Starting Out

1 Our Rainbow Magic Beginner Readers are perfect for first-time readers who are just beginning to develop reading skills and confidence. Approved by teachers, they contain a full range of educational levelling, as well as lively full-colour illustrations.

Developing Readers

2 Rainbow Magic Early Readers contain longer stories and wider vocabulary for building stamina and growing confidence. These are adaptations of our most popular Rainbow Magic stories, specially developed for younger readers in conjunction with an Early Years reading consultant, with full-colour illustrations.

Going Solo

3 The Rainbow Magic chapter books – a mixture of series and one-off specials – contain accessible writing to encourage your child to venture into reading independently. These highly collectible and much-loved magical stories inspire a love of reading to last a lifetime.

www.rainbowmagicbooks.co.uk

"Rainbow Magic got my daughter reading chapter books. Great sparkly covers, cute fairies and traditional stories full of magic that she found impossible to put down" – Mother of Edie (6 years)

"Florence LOVES the Rainbow Magic books. She really enjoys reading now" – Mother of Florence (6 years)

The Rainbow Magic Reading Challenge

Well done, fairy friend – you have completed the book!
This book was worth 5 points.

See how far you have climbed on the
Reading Rainbow opposite.

The more books you read, the more points you will get,
and the closer you will be to becoming a Fairy Princess!

How to get your Reading Rainbow
1. Cut out the coin below
2. Go to the Rainbow Magic website
3. Download and print out your poster
4. Add your coin and climb up the Reading Rainbow!

There's all this and lots more at
www.rainbowmagicbooks.co.uk

You'll find activities, competitions, stories, a special
newsletter and complete profiles of all the
Rainbow Magic fairies. Find a fairy with your name!